THE BLACKSMITH

THE BLACKSMITH

Tales from the Graveyard, Pt. 1

SUSAN SHULTZ

Susan Shultz

Loneliness and despair can be crippling, especially to the young. In some cases, they can be a gift, as they drive us inside ourselves to create an alternate world. Sometimes that world can be a nightmare. Sometimes it can be a magical kingdom.

I am grateful to my family and friends for their support throughout those experiences, from then to now, and during the writing of these stories.

Despair can be a window. Loneliness can lead to learning what your mind is capable of. Darkness can be devastating—but only if you let it.

Let me show you...

"The boundaries which divide Life from Death are at best shadowy and vague. Who shall say where the one ends, and where the other begins?"

"The Premature Burial" - Edgar Allan Poe

For Lucy Jane and Annabelle Lee, always

Prologue

I dreamed of you.

You came to me and took me in your arms, but your head was at my chest. I was the mother, the Madonna, your healer, your protector.

I held you to me, your head on my breasts, and I felt your warmth against me, my fingers in your hair. I breathed in your purity, your clean skin.

Your arms held me, wrapped around me tightly. We breathed together, and then held our breath in the silence.

You listened, your ear at my heart. I waited. We both heard nothing.

But can I still love?

I

A baby bird fell. It toppled from the nest and was caught in string its mother had gathered for nesting. Now it hangs from its mother's nest, rotting on a tiny gallows. It drifts in the breeze. Each day, it rots away more.

My name is Ainsley.
I live among the dead.

My grandmother left me this house. She died six years ago of ovarian cancer.

My father left us when I was born. My mother killed herself shortly after that. My grandmother raised me.

Behind my house is a graveyard. I spend much of my time there. I tend to the graves, to the dead things, like an anti-garden. To you, it may look somber. Dark.

To me, my graveyard is as beautiful as spring flowers, as fresh as ripe vegetables, ready for picking, mid-summer.

My heart is dead. It does not beat. It died some time ago.

Although it is dead, it feels hunger, like a zombie. It lurches on,

"

seeking heat, blood. Sometimes it feels pain. The pain in my heart is the spot where a broken bone, long healed, still aches when it rains.

My grandmother's house is on a hill set back from the road in a sleepy New England town. The driveway is hidden. No one can find us up here. There was a time, when I was younger, when our isolation frightened me. If a murderer were to break in with a hatchet, I'd be bleeding and dead long before any police could save me. No one would hear my screams.

Now, I love being far away from everyone. It seems appropriate. I want to be left alone with my thoughts and my graveyard. And my secrets.

The graveyard is way at the back of my large yard. The stones are very old and hard to read. I tend to the dead. There is grave dirt under my fingernails. My grandmother told me stories about those buried in the earth. I'm not sure if she actually researched any of it, or if they were fairy tales to keep me entertained. Fairy tales of death, of sorrow, and of pain. There was no fairy princess in these tales. No handsome prince.

The name of the family buried there is Brown.

Mother Brown hated her young daughter-in-law, my grandmother said. They fought for dominion over their small house.

The stress finally proved too much for the younger Mrs. Brown. According to her gravestone, she died at twenty-two, but not before giving birth to a child, who died an infant at two months. Poor Hubert tried to be a dutiful son as well as a devoted husband and father, but failed miserably at all three. He found himself caught in the middle between his mother and his young wife. After his wife died, my grandmother said, Hubert's mother got him back. All to herself.

Set apart from the Browns is another grave. I can barely make out the name on it, but it looks like *Bennett*. My grandmother told me Mr. Bennett was the family's blacksmith and friend.

The Blacksmith is my favorite. Sometimes, I sleep on his grave. Sometimes he visits me, in my dreams, both waking and sleeping. His hands are coarse from working with metal and heat. I like their hardness.

Don't give me tenderness. I don't need it. I love the Blacksmith's hardened hands, covered in calluses. I want him to seal off my insides with his glowing red poker. I want him to make me a suit of armor to cover my dead heart.

Some people claim they don't know why they kill.

I do it to feel warmth. To feel life. When you live among the dead, you start to miss that. The blood at the end of my knife looks like the red of iron after it's been cast on a fire. I can taste its heat.

I am thirty-eight years old. My ex-husband, Daniel, left me just after my second miscarriage, when the doctors told us I would never carry a child to term.

Even with fertility treatment, my body couldn't handle it.

He left me when I was thirty. Daniel came from money, and his family insisted on having an heir. So did he. He is full of himself. Daniel still sends me money now and then, and we visit together. I am not angry with him for leaving me when I needed him most; it can be convenient to have an almost-dead heart. Or was he the one who killed it? I try not to remember when my heart died because then I remember the pain. I don't want to remember that. And I don't want to remember when Daniel was my husband. I don't think Daniel remembered he was my husband even when he was.

After he left, I returned to my grandmother's house. It's where I belong. My graveyard friends welcomed me. I couldn't see them, but I knew they were smiling.

I met Daniel in my early twenties. Daniel was an up-and-coming stockbroker. I was an administrative assistant, attending college at night to get my master's in library science. He was charming, and I was stupid. Our marriage was unhappy. There were other women. My time with Daniel had already killed many things inside of me before the miscarriages came.

Daniel remarried quickly, as I expected him to. He now has four beautiful, blond children—two daughters and twin sons. His wife is lovely. She sends me a Christmas card from their family every year. She doesn't mind Daniel, and so she belongs with him.

My hair is brown. I dress simply. I try to blend in with the walls most of the time. You might have seen me once somewhere, but I'm sure you don't remember it.

On my knees, I pull weeds from the dirt by the graves. My grave-yard garden is perfect. Healthy grass, spots of lavender. I scattered step-stones throughout the graves, and there is a bench for me to sit on as I read or write poems for Sam. I'll tell you more about him later.

Beyond the stones, there are other graves. They are unmarked.

Only the Blacksmith knows who they are.

2

I work in the library three days a week. I don't need the money. Between what my grandmother left me and what Daniel gives me, I am comfortable. But I still work because love books. They don't talk. Out loud, at least.

Portia is my boss. She is sweet but nosy about my life. She thinks I need to date. I don't need to date. I don't want to date. Portia is older than me by about twenty years. She has grandchildren who she doesn't see very often. Her son lives in another state, so I often get the leftovers of her untapped maternal urges. Pushing up her glasses, she studies me, with a grimace, like a fiction book put back into the self-help section.

"Ainsley, you look tired. Why don't you take a long lunch?"

"Thank you, Portia. I'm fine. I brought my lunch, but maybe I will sit outside and read in the sun."

"Are you sure you're feeling all right? You look pale."

Oh, Portia. You're so sweet. But get off my back.

"I'm fine, thank you." I turn and go about my work, sorting and stacking in the peace and quiet. Trying to keep away from her prying comments.

"Why do you always dress in such dark colors, Ainsley?"

Because I'm hoping to hide from you and anyone else interested in my business.

I don't say this. That would be mean.

"You could use some color. You're still a young woman. Brighten yourself up. Find a boyfriend. I worry about you up in that house by yourself all the time."

"I don't want a boyfriend, Portia. I want to be left alone." I say this in my nicest but firmest way.

Portia gets the hint.

I enjoy my peace for a bit until I hear her singsong voice interrupting me again.

"Ainsley, Sam is here!"

This time, I don't mind the interruption. She is probably happier to see Sam than I am.

She says she still carries a torch for the two of us. I never tell anyone of the secret fire I carry.

Sam has been my friend since high school. We dated briefly, but it never went anywhere. Some might call it puppy love. It was an innocent type of thing. He still calls me by my high school nickname.

"Hey, A.J. How's it going? Let's go outside and have lunch."

If I could feel love, I'd say I might be in love with Sam. Instead, I am just obsessed. I've been obsessed for almost twenty years, give or take. We lost touch when he spent several years traveling for work. But he moved back a few years ago, conveniently, after Daniel and I divorced. It was good timing for me. I needed someone. I still do.

Sam has always been my angel. Even in my darkest times I know he is always beside me, like he was when the other A was lost to me. He inspires my good side. He still helps me believe, sometimes, that I have the potential for wholesome happiness. Truthfully, I'm not ready to entirely give up on that, although the Blacksmith tells me my time is near. Sam looks a little bit like my Blacksmith. Their eyes are very similar. Other than the fact that one is dead.

I wonder what our baby would look like. Would he have their eyes?

I am good at hiding my obsession. I maintain control even when Sam tells me about all his dates. He even tells me about the ones he has sex with, and how it is. I dig my fingernails into my palm, and I can keep smiling. Luckily, when Sam talks about things like that, he barely pauses to see if I have anything to say or if I'm even paying attention. That's the way Sam is sometimes.

Someone watching us would never know the merciless razor of jealousy ripping through my insides. Sometimes, I dig my nails into my palm so hard I bleed. I pretend that the skin of my palm is the girl's neck. That helps me smile.

Sam doesn't get it. He treats me like I'm just one of the guys. I'm all right with that as long as he stays around. I'd rather him be oblivious than have him leave my side. Or think of me as some kind of crazy stalker. Which I'm not.

I'm not crazy.

Am I?

"So, how's your garden coming along?" Sam gestures to the dirt under my fingernails.

His hair is brown and wavy. He has dark eyes, like my Blacksmith's. Dark and shiny, like metal.

But Sam is not dead. He is definitely alive. Sometimes I think that is why I'm so attracted to him. My coldness reaches for his warmth, his flame. Everyone loves Sam. I take what I can get.

"Not bad."

"Why don't I ever get any tomatoes? You're always tending that garden, and I never see any of it."

I smile. Sam is cute.

"I don't grow tomatoes. You probably wouldn't want anything that I grow." "Well, maybe I'd know that if I ever came over. But you never invite me."

I bite my lip when he isn't looking. We are sitting out on the library steps in the sun. Where Sam belongs. His hair shines in the sun. His laughter is summer. The sun hurts my eyes. It makes them weep hot tears.

"You can come over any time you want. You know that."

"Well, maybe one of these days, I'll take you up on it. I want to see this famous garden of yours."

I would love to show Sam my garden. I can show him the places where I have slept among the graves and the places where I have done things. Bad things. While thinking about him.

If anyone could understand, it's Sam. But I am not quite ready to take that chance.

3

My library clothes are very conservative. They cover what I keep buried. I even wear those cliché librarian glasses. I pull my hair back. I don't like high heels. That's how I like to dress. It used to make my grandmother so angry.

"You're such a pretty girl. Why do you hide under all those clothes?"

Because I like to hide, grandmother. There are ugly things within me that no one should ever see.

"Fix your hair. Put on some makeup."

I didn't always dress that way. When I met my ex-husband, I dressed to show my body more. But even then, I never dressed the way I do now, when I go out at night.

Despite all my hiding, I do like to go out some nights. I never know when I'll be in the mood. Most of the time, I am content to stay among the dead. Among the whispering ghosts and the cold, crumbling stone. Other nights, I can't take the silence. The loneliness. Thoughts of Sam drive me into the night.

I wear all black. Short, short skirts. Fishnet stockings. Knee-high boots. Lace shirts or other see-through things.

I put on makeup.

I use liquid eyeliner to trace thick, black lines around my eyes. I spread blush over my cheeks. I paint my mouth a shiny, cherry red. My grandmother used to say that girls who wear red on their lips are trying to make boys think of other body parts. I'm okay with that.

I live within walking distance of the train, so I head there and get on the next train out. My money is tucked into my red lace bra.

The train ride is short. Some men look at me. I look back. I'm not shy in this outfit. I'm a different person. Another Ainsley. An Ainsley that not even Sam would recognize.

Portia might have fainted.

At my stop, I get off the train and head to the nearest nightclub. I pay my cover charge. A loud band is playing awful music. I hate it. But this is where I need to be right now.

It doesn't take long. I have my drink in hand and am shimmying along with the music when a young man approaches me. I can already tell he is an arrogant one.

Perfect.

"Hey, gorgeous. Want to dance?"
"Sure."

We move our bodies together for a while. His name is Paul. He just started a job in the area. He lives in a nearby apartment with a roommate. Paul brags that he comes from money. That his job is amazing. That he is going to buy a Porsche once he makes his first million, which he expects to do by thirty.

Paul is over ten years younger than I am, but he either doesn't know or doesn't care. I have a feeling he doesn't notice much about anyone but himself. Paul is starting to remind me of my ex-husband. The Blacksmith has told me to feed my anger. Let it take over. Give in to this hate. This rage.

Tonight is working out perfectly.

I touch Paul a lot. I touch his arm. I touch his knee. I laugh at all of his jokes. The next song comes on, and Paul stays seated in a barstool. I turn my back to him and dance between his legs, moving my body against his. His hands are on my hips. When I can't see him, I pretend his hands are Sam's.

Most of the time when I pick guys up, I pretend they are Sam.

Sometimes, if they are really rough, I imagine that my Blacksmith has taken over their bodies with his spirit. I look deeply into their eyes and I see him there. He is strong and protective. He possesses me. He owns me. He has branded me.

Then I do something for him—my Blacksmith.

Paul leans into my ear.

"Let's get the fuck out of here."

He takes my hand and leads me through the crowded bar and out the front door.

"How did you get here?"

"I took the train. I don't live that far from here by car. And I live alone..."

"Sweet, let's go."

I look at Paul as we drive. He is relatively handsome. Not my type. Too fair, too blond. Too Fairfield County: arrogant, entitled, golf playing, summer home owning, ass-grabbing douchebag.

He has the look of an aristocrat, condescending to consort with a lucky, chosen peasant. It would never occur to Paul that I could be anything but thrilled by his attentions. He thinks he chose me.

Actually, I chose him.

"Have you ever been in love, Paul?"

"Have I? Uh. I don't know. I guess so."

"You would know if you had been in love."

"How about you?"

"My heart doesn't work properly anymore."

He looks at me, as if for the first time. But he is too horny to turn back now. I direct Paul up my driveway. The road is dark and bumpy.

"Shit, you live up here by yourself? Aren't you scared?"

I have my protector in the backyard. But he doesn't need to know that.

"I'm used to it. I've lived here all my life." I pause. "Why? Are you?" I smile. He laughs, a little nervously.

We stop on the patio, and I tell him to wait outside in the summer evening. I grab two bottles of beer and come back outside.

"Let's go up to the backyard. I want to show you something."

"Up there?" He hesitantly gestures into the darkness.

I kiss him then, tongue first, hard. His hands grab my ass tightly. I pull away.

"Don't you want to see what I have to show you? Come on. We'll play hide and seek." I run into the dark.

Paul runs after me, laughing. "Hey, wait!"

I run to my graveyard garden. I light the candles and wait on the bench. Paul finds me quickly, following the flickering light.

"Oh...spooky. Are you one of those Goth chicks? I should have known by the way you were dressed. Still, this is," he gestures to my graveyard, "pretty cool."

He sits next to me, and I give him a beer

I drink mine fast.

 rise and move to stand over my Blacksmith's grave. I open the buttons of my lace shirt. I unzip my skirt and kick it off. I stand in the candlelight, wearing just my red lace bra and panties, with my garters holding up my fishnets and my boots. It is quite the presentation, or so I've been told.

Paul puts his beer down. He stands and walks over to me.

"Wow." He kisses me like I kissed him earlier. No love. All tongue.

His hands move all over my body, pulling my bra down, pulling off my panties.

"You're not going to sacrifice me or anything, are you? Because if so, I'm not a virgin." He laughs.

I just smile at him.

I pull him to the ground. His head rests beside a headstone. I pull at his clothes until he is naked and climb on top of him. When he is deep inside me, his eyes close, and his head sinks back.

Then I slit his throat.

His eyes open wide in shock for a second, but it's over very soon. I've become so skilled. Naked, I work in the candlelight, cutting Paul into pieces. I am covered in his blood. It warms me on the outside. I lick my fingers and feel his life warm me on the inside.

Finally, I find his heart.

Eating a human heart is harder than you think.

It is a muscle, strong and tough. I eat what I can. Enough to fill me with life and heat. I lick the blood off my fingers. I wonder what my own heart would taste like, all bitter and dead. Probably not a fit meal for anyone.

I get my shovel. I roll my wheelbarrow over to what remains of Paul.

I must look quite a sight in my fishnets and boots, covered in blood, rolling a wheelbarrow across the yard in the moonlight.

I roll pieces of his body to the area behind the graveyard, where I have planted patches of flowers over previously disturbed areas of earth. It looks so pretty.

There are hydrangeas and even a lilac tree. I am hoping to put in more black-eyed Susans and daisies. Maybe a sunflower or two. They look cheerful.

I start to dig. My arms are used to burying things. But then again, so is my head.

When I'm finished, I'm sticky and dirty and exhausted. I grab Paul's warm beer and sit with my Blacksmith, telling him about my evening. He smiles and fires up the coals.

My anger feeds his fire. My blood feeds his need for me. I'm getting closer. He knows that.

I sleep.

4

Today, I stay home and clean.

I shower for almost an hour after waking up in the graveyard.

I always do after a night like that.

Sam tries to call me, but I can't talk to him. I feel that familiar mix of shame and satisfaction that no one would ever understand. Not even Sam.

I mop the kitchen floor three times. I scrub the bathtub until my fingers are raw. I strip the bed. I do all the laundry. I nap for a while. After my nap, I take Paul's car back to the bar parking lot.

Paul's car is fast. Too fast. I enjoy the ride. After being certain I have left nothing of myself behind, I take the train back home again, an entirely different Ainsley now.

After dinner, I put on *Night of the Living Dead*. It is one of my favorite horror movies of all time. I can relate to the monsters.

I sympathize with their hunger. Their lives are so simple. No matter what the obstacle, they lurch forward, seeking to fill their emptiness. Their loved ones look at them as strangers. They move in packs, but each has a lonely existence.

I think about Sam. In some ways, the zombies' hunger reminds me of how I feel about him. All they want are brains. They are fixated on them. All they say is "Brains, brains, brains." They'll do anything for brains.

I love Sam the way a zombie loves brains.

Horror movies are therapeutic for me. I feel healed and renewed after watching them. Fear is so pure. I love to be afraid. It is thrilling.

I always relate to the wrong characters. Like Jason in *Friday the 13th*. Or Michael Myers in *Halloween*; especially Michael Myers. I feel an almost sexual attraction to him. There's something about his patient walk. His big knife that he draws without taking no as an answer.

There's something hot in submitting to the inevitable.

5

I spend some time talking to the younger Mrs. Brown in the graveyard.

Poor thing. She died so young and had such a difficult life. Her mother-in-law hated her.

She was just a young woman in an unfriendly and unhealthy household. All she wanted was a baby to love.

Mother Brown would spill things on her freshly laundered clothing. She would turn up the flame on the stew simmering for her husband's dinner. She tried to stick up for herself, but Mother Brown was a formidable woman.

When she had the baby, things got worse. Mother Brown would pinch the baby when she walked by, causing the poor infant to scream and fuss.

Mother Brown was always telling her son what a poor wife and mother he had chosen. Mrs. Brown's husband always deferred to his mother. Soon his mother's bullying got the best of both of them. They started to fight. The baby got crankier.

Then, Mother Brown killed their baby boy.

Of course, the young Mrs. Brown had no way to prove this. She sits, silently weeping on the bench next to me, holding her ghost baby. They are transparent, but they are more alive than I am.

At least they can love.

Late one night, she put the baby to sleep in her cradle. Mrs. Brown was exhausted from doing and redoing chores all day, and she fell asleep next to the cradle. She slept deeply.

When she woke, the sun was high. It felt wrong somehow. Her baby lay unmoving in her crib. In the night he had pulled the pillow over his face and suffocated. Or, someone had smothered him.

Mrs. Brown screamed and screamed. She fell to the floor and prayed God would take her instead.

Mother Brown stood at the doorway, a smirk hidden in her expressionless face.

Mr. Brown shunned his young wife from then on. At the baby's burial, he stood at his mother's side, leaving her to grieve alone, in silence and shame.

But Mother Brown, after destroying her son's marriage and isolating her daughter-in-law, was not satisfied yet.

She told anyone who would listen that her daughter-in-law's laziness and neglect had caused her grandson's death. All the elders of the town patted the old woman's hand.

Young Mrs. Brown was ignored. Or clucked at disapprovingly. She took to staying home alone in her room. She ate less.

She found solace only in the Blacksmith, visiting him as he worked. She liked the sound of the clanging metal. The spray of fire. He did not talk to her. But he did not look at her with disgust. He just worked. And sometimes, he listened.

The younger Mrs. Brown eventually died, alone in her attic room. No one found her for a week. Mother Brown and Mr. Brown had not noticed she was gone. Or they had known, but didn't care.

But after death, she was reunited with her son.

I ask her what it's like to have a baby, and what it feels like to love a child. I want to know what it's like to be a mother. My ovaries are as empty as my heart.

I tell her about my broken womb. My babies also died, but inside of me. For this, she is able to find some sympathy in her heart for me. I think she can sense my isolation.

She holds out her baby son for me to take in my arms. I hesitate.

Then I take him. I hold the gurgling baby. He is so happy to be reunited with his mother that he even shares a smile with me.

And I cry. For the first time in many years. Tears drip heavily from my eyes, through my ghostly charge, and into the dirt below.

The things buried there will never grow.

6

Last night I dreamt I ate Sam.

The emptiness inside me was like a hot air balloon, filling me from head to toe.

Nothing could invade that emptiness.

I felt my heart. It died for certain years ago, but in my dream I could feel it again. It was hanging on for dear life. Kicking and screaming. Trying to get me to do something, anything, to relieve its pain.

My heart was no stranger to pain. In fact, the existence my heart knew, before its death, was of more pain than pleasure. Even pleasure itself was painful because it was so fleeting. I tried to hang onto it.

Feeling pleasure is like wearing your little sister's wedding dress. You know it isn't your size. You can look in the mirror in faded light, but it won't ever fit you or be yours. Eventually, you have to take it off.

If your heart's dead, are you really alive? I don't know what a soul is anymore, but if I had one, I'm sure that it's dead, too.

So I dreamt of eating Sam. Biting through his flesh, his bones, his organs. Feeling his blood wash down my face. Swallowing the life that I can't have. We were together, for a while. I owned him.

I dreamt I issued my invitation formally, through a note.

I dreamt I put out my clothing for our dinner. The oven was cold because I was not cooking anything.

I wanted Sam raw and warm.

I didn't want anything to affect the taste of his blood running down my throat. I wanted his heart to pulse and beat while I chewed. I wanted his life inside of me. Maybe it would warm me for a few minutes.

You can't tell I'm dead just by looking at me. I still look normal. I'm not one of those *Night of the Living Dead* zombies, all caked up and bruised and glazed over. My eyes are not dead. My skin looks alive. Looking alive makes me more dangerous.

I am a monster in disguise. Sam doesn't know to run from me.

No, the only thing that's twisted and ugly about me is something you can't see. My heart. Its jaw opens hungrily for living flesh. It's malformed and starting to decompose, rotting. It groans with a hunger for all that lives. No one can see that, though.

I dressed in a fine evening gown. I had much to celebrate. Sam would be mine, finally. The long black gown hugged my body. My makeup was exquisite. Full red lips and dark, Cleopatra eyes. I was the seductress. The temptress. Come closer.

As the time approached for our dinner, I grew excited to see Sam.

Excited to kill him.

Excited to eat him, slowly.

I don't hate Sam. My zombie heart, that grinning, dead thing, was in charge of the feelings department. When it died, my emotions died with it. Now, I'm just hungry. I'm driven by my biological needs alone.

Once, those needs might have included kissing Sam. Fucking Sam. Now, they just involve chewing Sam until he slides down my throat.

In my dream, my only dilemma was whether I should keep Sam alive while I ate him. If he remained alive, I'd need to incapacitate him. That could be fun. I decided to see how the mood struck me.

The doorbell rang at seven thirty. Sam was due at seven o'clock. I was relieved when he showed up.

Sam arrived at the door bearing roses and his effortless charm.

If my heart still lived, it might have been tempted to let him live. But, my heart is dead. And hungry.

Dream Sam was suitably impressed by my gown.

I showed him to the couch and got him a drink. I fawned over him appropriately so that he suspected nothing. I sat demurely before him. He was so trusting, like always.

Sam asked me what was for dinner.

"You," I answered without missing a beat. He smiled.

In my dream, I finally decided it would be best to have Sam alive, but not awake. I wanted his heart beating when I started eating him. He was still smiling when I knocked him unconscious with the cast iron pan I had hidden behind my back.

I didn't bother with an apron before making the first incision. He started to bleed. I used my big butcher knife. That cast iron pan was really hard. Sam was probably dying. But not yet. He was still breathing.

I tasted Sam's blood on my fingers. I felt such a rush, finally swallowing him, owning him.

I am experienced with finding the heart, even in my dreams. I want to eat that most of all. I tasted Sam's skin and his blood, and I will eat the other parts of him. But then, I wanted his heart.

When my heart was alive, he wouldn't give his to me. I couldn't ask for it.

I cut out a large part of the heart, and brought it to my lips. His blood was up to my elbows, and all over my face. My gown was trashed.

I was crying, but I didn't know why. I didn't feel anything: a ghoul, feeding my hunger.

As I swallowed a large part of it, I felt it stick in my throat. Perhaps a sob had caught it. Maybe it was too big to fit down my gullet.

I started to choke. My hands went to my throat as my oxygen was cut off. I was choking on Sam's warm heart.

My brain started to go black and join my heart in death.

My last thought, just before I choked to death and before I woke up, was that Sam had finally killed me. All of me.

7

I work in a library because it's quiet. Books don't talk back. Portia likes to talk, but I can hide among the shelves and drown her out.

I have always loved books. When I was a small child, I would sneak any form of light I could find into my room and read as late as I could.

Because books are alive. They are more alive than you and me. Books live forever. They live on in their own jackets. They live on in the reader's memory. They live on in their writers' minds.

I can enter the world of Emily Dickinson. I relate to her. I read her poetry and am transported to a garden in Amherst, Mass. I visited her grave once. And I talked with her as only I can talk to the dead. I took an etching of her gravestone to keep with me.

I framed it and hung it in my bedroom.

I descend into the depths of Edgar Allan Poe and Annabel Lee, his black cat driving him to madness. Or I lose myself in the magical and gothic worlds of Shirley Jackson.

I sort the books and feel their covers. I run my fingers through their words. I flip through the pages. If I'm quiet, I can hear them whispering to me without words, tugging at my insides, calling me, seducing me into their world, opening themselves to me and inviting me inside.

I am satisfied to be paid to swim in an ocean of books. They are my friends. When they need something, I am glad to provide it.

Since I am having dinner after work with Sam, I take extra care with my appearance. I brush my dark hair back from my face, and I put on a bit of makeup. I wear an oversized light sweater and jeans. Sam wouldn't know what to do with anything else. And my glasses, of course. Always my glasses.

He is right on time, pulling up in his convertible with the top down. So much for combing my hair.

"Hey, A.J.! Get in. I hope you're hungry."

"I'm starving."

At the casual restaurant, he orders us some beers. We sit outside in the sun.

My dead heart lurches as I gaze at his soft hair and his eyes catching the light. Sam belongs in the sun.

"A.J., you're too pale. You spend too much time stuck in that crummy library. You need to come to the beach with me sometime, or go hiking or something. Get out. Get some fresh air."

I know he's speaking out of genuine concern. So I like it.

"I'm fine, Sam. How was your date?" I want to get this part of our conversation over with.

"Honestly? I think I'm in love for the first time, A.J."

My insides split with the precision of a goring hook that has been jabbed into my abdomen and yanked out again. Each word in that sentence is the prong of a pitchfork thrust in my entrails. I blink very fast, tilting my head back to finish my beer and get myself together.

Luckily, once Sam gets going, he doesn't stop for a breath.

"She's amazing. Gorgeous. And so funny. You would really like her."

close my eyes for a second to ride this pain out like a wave. I remind myself it is only a phantom pain, grazing by where my heart used to be. I feel it like an amputee feels an ache in his missing leg.

"Are you all right?" He reaches out to touch my arm. I pull away more sharply than I mean to.

"I'm fine. I just felt the beginning of a migraine coming on."

I pretend to look in my purse for some aspirin. By the time I look up, I have the mask back on. Instant, perfect friend. Just add alcohol.

"So you were saying?"

"Are you sure you're okay?" He sounds confused.

"Yes, yes. I'm fine. Tell me more about your one true love you met yesterday." "Ha, funny. Actually, I've known her for a while. She works with me. But this was only our second date. Or was it third?"

"Oh. Has she passed the ultimate Sam test?" Sam has a theory that he can only really know a girl if he sleeps with her. Bad experiences in the past.

"She did." Sam smiled and blushes.

I'm not going to make it through this dinner. I snap at the waiter for another beer.

"Wow! You finished that fast!"

Yeah, no kidding.

"You already slept with her? That's fast for you." Why am I torturing myself? "I know. It just sort of happened. We couldn't help it."

The waiter returns. "Are you ready to order?"

"I'll have a cheeseburger and fries. How about you, A.J.?"

I'm already full.

"I'll have a small house salad. And another one of these." I hold up the beer.

"And a shot of tequila."

"That's all you're eating? I thought you were hungry. And a shot of tequila?

What's up with you tonight?"

"I'm fine. Go ahead, tell me more." I'd rather him talking than focused on me.

"Well, we were out dancing, and she kissed me. I didn't expect it, but it was an amazing kiss. Just amazing. Everything clicked. You know how that is?"

I nod as I take another sip of beer. Under the table, my fingernails are digging into my palm, helping me to keep the smile on.

"When I dropped her off, she invited me in. The next thing I knew, she was on my lap on the couch. And that was it. It just went from there. I didn't plan on doing it that soon, but it seemed right."

"Ah."

"Do you think I made a mistake?" He seems genuinely concerned about my opinion.

"Well, Sam, it's pretty easy to feel like you're in love with a girl who's willing to give you a blow job and fall into the sack with you on the second date. But, hey, I think it's good that you're lowering your standards."

"Hey!"

Oh well, fuck it.

"What? I'm telling you the truth. If you want a lie, go somewhere else. You're the one who always wants to give it some time before you have sex so as not to cloud your judgment. You've decided to lower that standard. Good for you. We're all allowed to change. And she could be a really nice girl. But I wouldn't start picking out china. You're still in that after-sex high."

"You're right." But he looks less happy than when he first arrived.

I feel awful. I want Sam to be happy. Even if he isn't happy with me. Don't I?

"I'm sorry, sweetie," I force myself to say. "I'm not trying to rain on your parade. I can see that you're happy. And you should be. It sounds like you had a great night. I just want you to keep that wariness that I love about you. Be cautiously happy."

I could be up for an Academy Award at this point.

"I'm only saying this because I care. You're an excellent catch."

He smiles at me. I'm in the shade, but I suddenly feel warm all over.

"I know, A.J."

I hold my beer out and toast him.

"And, yes, I realize you are surprised that I know how girls think. Being that you don't remember I'm a girl most of the time." I roll my eyes as I take a drink.

He laughs.

"Trust me, A.J., I always remember that you're a girl. Always." He winks at me.

And just like that, my starving heart finds something to eat.

After dinner, I'm pretty drunk. Sam walks me to the car, arm in arm.

"I thought you used to be able to hold your liquor?" Sam is laughing.

"How else could I get you to walk me to the car like a gentleman?" I say.

"All you ever need to do is ask me, A.J. I'll do most anything you ask me to."

He opens the passenger door for me.

We drive the short distance to my house, and he shuts the lights off.

"It's so dark. I don't know how you live up here by yourself. Why don't you sell

this place and get an apartment somewhere?"

"I love my house. I love the dark. Plus, there's my garden. Who would take care of it?" I put my head on his shoulder.

That's right. I guess it's too dark to see it now?"

I think quietly about the dirt piles up there.

"Not now, I'm too tired. I'd probably fall on a rose bush."

He laughs.

"You're a funny girl, A.J. You know that?"

"That's my goal. To be the girl everyone describes as having a great sense of humor."

He laughs again.

He ruffles his fingers through my hair and pulls me off his shoulder. Sam looks into my eyes for a minute. He takes my glasses off.

"Why don't you get contacts? You have such pretty eyes," he said.

"Is that a line you used on your girl from last night?"

I'm getting nervous. I don't know where this is going. My insides are still aching. I can't handle it.

"Can you stop making wisecracks for one minute?" he said.

We look at each other for a moment.

"What?" I ask, nervously. I feel my walls going up.

"I just wanted to look at you. No one would ever say you're the girl with the great sense of humor. Although you do have one. They'd say that you are the girl with the golden hazel eyes." He touches my hair for a second.

"Who doesn't realize how beautiful she really is, inside and out, and hides herself up in this little house on a hill in the dark. A.J., you have a beautiful heart. You should let yourself out of your prison sometimes."

Oh, Sam. My heart isn't beautiful. It's dead.

"Sam..." I stroke his cheek for second.

Then I remember about the girl from last night. The one he's in love with. I can't believe I let my guard down like this.

"Thanks for dinner."

For a second, Sam looks slightly confused. And hurt. Then he kisses my forehead.

"Goodnight, A.J."

I leave him in the dark with his questions.

I sleep on my Blacksmith's grave that night with my fingers buried in the dirt and my cheek kissed by his rocky soil.

8

I get up late this morning for my meeting with Daniel. I'm supposed to meet him at nine o'clock at the diner. Maybe it's psychological. Trying to protect myself.

Daniel isn't mean or violent, he just blatantly doesn't care about me. I am only a blip in his perfect history. He didn't even call me to make the appointment. He had his secretary do it.

I tried to kill Daniel once. Or at least, I thought so hard about it that I came very close to doing it. I thought about poisoning him. I thought about stabbing him. I even thought that all the hormone treatments and the miscarriage might make for a good alibi. Finally, I decided he wasn't worth the jail time.

He would have tasted as bland as his personality.

But if I had known for certain I could get away with it, I would have done it. Daniel's net worth would have made me a suspect immediately. Even though I never cared about his money. I just wanted him to love me.

I pull into the crowded diner parking lot and give myself a pep talk. I try to make myself appear that I feel I am worthy and in- telligent. That I think I matter. He may have won, but I still want to retain some of my dignity. That's what I have to do before seeing my ex-husband.

He is there already, and I see him look at his watch as I walk through the door. "Still punctual as ever, I see."

"Hello, Daniel."

"Please, sit." He gestures to the other bench. He snaps to get the server's attention.

"Another coffee, please?" He points to me. "You're not hungry, are you?"

He looks very handsome. Tan. Probably from being out on his sailboat. His blue eyes are bright but cold. He wears a golf shirt.

"No, I'm not hungry."

"Good. I don't have a lot of time. I have a meeting on the golf course in an hour, and with rush hour traffic—"

"What do you need me to sign, Daniel?"

"Oh, uh, right." He rustles through his papers.

"Here, just some estate stuff. Thanks." He passes some papers to me, and I have them all signed in a few minutes.

"You're looking good." I know he's lying. He's barely looked at me. "Thanks. So are you. You got some sun."

"The kids love the boat. It's great."

"How is Margaret? And the family?"

"They're doing great, thanks."

He runs through various community activities and volunteer positions and charity balls and kids' sports activities while I quietly drink my coffee. Eventually, I interrupt him.

"Don't you have to go?" I point at my watch.

"Oh, shit. Yeah. Right. Thanks. You may not be able to keep track of time, but somehow you're still keeping me organized! Wait, uh. How is...I mean, how are you?"

"I'm the same, Daniel. The same. Have a good meeting. Take care." I try to sound cheerful as I let him off the hook.

With a look of relief, he breezes back out into the world of Daniel, leaving me to drink my coffee in solitude.

Selfish bastard.

The first time I talked to the dead, I was twelve years old.

My best friend died of a heart condition in seventh grade. She and I had been inseparable. Our walk to and from school led us through a graveyard, and we would walk in between the stones, daring each other to stand on unknown graves.

We'd make up stories about the names on the stones, sometimes ghostly stories of revenge, and sometimes nicer stories. We'd marvel over the ones that looked ancient, and we'd stare in fascination at the freshly buried.

Her name began with an A too, so we'd be the A team, or some other variation of A's to the kids in school. I used to always get in trouble for taking too long to walk home. But those were magical times. It was the last time I can really ever remember feeling truly weightless. No stones to carry around inside.

The other A was always sick, but I didn't think anything of it in my twelve- year-old mind. Then one day she went to the hospital, and my grandmother came to get me at school.

I remember the walk to the principal's office in cheesy-movie slow motion. I see my classmates laughing, oblivious to my path, but their voices sound slowed- down. I see my grandmother in the sunlight by the office window.

I hear my grandmother saying that A is dead. I hear my own screams separate from myself. I returned home from school that day with a veil over my eyes. It never lifted, only got darker.

The other A was the first dead person I ever saw. My grandmother walked me into the funeral home. As we got to the door, I saw her in her pink-lined coffin. She was wearing her confirmation dress, and she had her ring on.

I had a matching ring, the one with the diamond "A." I stopped in shock. I tried to run away, but my grandmother stopped me.

"Don't be so selfish. Look at her mother. She is watching you. Waiting for you."

The other A was buried in our cemetery. I walked home by myself, but she was still with me. Now, I did not visit any other graves. Only hers. I sat on the pile of freshly dug earth. Her family had fashioned a temporary wooden cross that was stuck crudely in the ground.

We would sit and talk for hours. My grandmother would finally come looking for me and lead me home for dinner. My fingers were always covered in dirt.

I had already started watching horror movies. The other A and I used to watch them together before she died. *Night of the Living Dead* was my favorite, even then. And that was before I had buried my best friend and started to wake up in the middle of night, imagining her rotting away.

I imagined I could see the cemetery from my bedroom window. I imagined, as I looked out my window in the dark, that I could faintly see the other A shuffling up our long driveway in the darkness. I could see her in her white confirmation dress, wearing her matching ring. I imagined the other A was lonely in the cemetery.

I tried to talk to the other A from my bedroom. I told her I would spend as much time as I could with her. I pleaded with her to not dig her way out of the grave and come for me.

I had nightmares about the other A rotting in the ground. I imagined her eyes white and glazed. Her mouth open. I lost so much sleep that my grandmother took me to the doctor for sedatives.

Had it not been for Sam, back then, I probably would have ended up in the ground next to the other A. Sam was always there. I knew that. But even Sam could not penetrate the bitter moat of tears I had surrounded myself with.

I walked around school with dirty hands and circles under my eyes, either in a stupor from no sleep or a stupor from sedatives. I would not allow anyone to sit in the other A's empty desk. If someone tried to, I made a huge scene. Her desk stayed empty the rest of the year.

My grades fell. I stayed that way until I finished eighth grade. My school allowed me to graduate by the skin of my teeth. Part of me feels that they just wanted me out of there.

All I did was remind them of death.

10

Tonight, I sit in the graveyard and think of Sam. Poor Sam, always hoping to get a tomato from my dead garden.

Sam is the only person I can come close to loving. He has never hurt me intentionally. He has never left me intentionally. His eyes are so like my Blacksmith's. And he does not know me as the monster I am. I was not so nice to Sam the last time we were together. He deserves better than me. He is a good friend. If Sam can love me, in any way, perhaps I'm not all monster inside.

I fight myself over my feelings for Sam. How can I be a good friend and be jealous? How can I get angry with him when he dates other women? All I want is what is best for Sam. I could be a wonderful wife to him. I could mother his babies.

I talk to my Blacksmith about it. And I know I'm delusional thinking that.

I ask him why I can't just tell Sam how I feel. My Blacksmith shows me the earth behind the graveyard. He asks how I can ever hope to have a future with someone like Sam, who belongs in the sun, when I belong in the dark. In the dirt.

My Blacksmith is right.

But, I ask, what if I tell Sam everything? What if I come clean and tell him all the things I've done?

My Blacksmith says that if I tell Sam, I will lose the little that I have of him. He will think I am a monster. He will leave me forever. He will be disgusted by me, and I will die alone in jail.

If I am quiet, I will still have part of Sam. And I will always have my Blacksmith. And the dead. I will never be alone here.

But sometimes, the dirt isn't enough when I want to be held in Sam's arms. When I want him to tell me everything is going to be all right. Sometimes, it just isn't enough.

I ask the Blacksmith how I can ever stop this hunger in my dead heart.

He tells me I have to feed my heart. I don't want to listen to my Blacksmith, but I know he's right. He sees me for all I am, every part. And he accepts and cares for all of me. He wants me, even. Every step brings me closer to him.

I don't want to think about it.

11

Tonight, I decide to go out.

I wear my black silk dress. It is short and sleeveless. I pile my brown hair on top of my head and paint my lips red, my eyes dark. I wear pink silk panties. And black shiny heels.

I hop on the train once again and head out into the night.

This bar is more crowded than the last one I went to. But the music is better.

I get myself a drink and sit at the bar, watching people. A guy catches my eye. This one is older than I am. He is cute.

Finally, he walks over to me. He isn't very steady on his feet, which is good.

For later.

"Hey, beautiful. Can I buy you a drink?"

"Sure." I smile at him.

He buys me a drink and puts his hand on my hip. I don't mind. I drink my drink and let this guy talk. I don't even ask his name. It isn't important. And he isn't interested in mine.

He keeps his hand on my hip. Normally, I make some attempt to get to know my lovers. But tonight I feel impatient.

After some senseless small talk, I ask the guy if he wants to go somewhere more private.

We push through the crowd and go outside where he pushes me into the wall and kisses me. He's sloppy and drunk. I can't even close my eyes and pretend he's Sam this time. It's that bad.

I push him off, but he persists. Suddenly, I hear someone calling me. "A.J.?"

I looked past drunk guy to see Sam. With a girl.

"A.J., is that you? Are you okay?"

I fill with rage at the sight of him. With her. I can't even see her. Rage covers my eyes with black.

"Sam! How nice to see you." My voice is cold. "I'm fine. Thanks for asking. And this is?" I gesture to the girl.

"This is…" His voice trails off as he takes in my outfit.

"This is Kelly. Kelly, this is my oldest and dearest friend, A.J. I've told you about her."

"Wow. A.J. I've heard so much about you." She is looking me up and down. I want to slap her. I dig my fingernails into my palm and decline her extended hand. I imagine digging them into her jugular vein.

"You look different than I expected."

"So do you," I say.

"Well, you two enjoy your night. We were just leaving." I take my companion, who is zoning out into the distance, by the hand and move him down the street. Sam catches me by the arm when I am a few steps away.

"A.J., who is this guy? He looks totally drunk. Where are you going with him? Why are you dressed this way?" He gestures to my outfit.

I rip my arm away from his grip.

"What the fuck do you care? Go back to your one true love." I hate myself for saying it, but I can't help it.

"A.J., wait. Don't do this! It's not safe."

Not safe for whom, I think.

"Let go." I make my voice as cold as I can. He lets go of my arm and walks away.

This poor drunk idiot doesn't know what he's in for. My rage is bitter, and my dead heart is hungry. We leave his car behind, and I drag him onto the train. Leave the questions near the bar. Not near my house. I learned that the hard way with Paul.

We get off the train. I have to shake him hard to wake him up. I drag him up the driveway and up the hill to the cemetery. He can barely walk. He collapses on my Blacksmith's grave.

Exhausted, I sit on the ground next to him. I kick off my heels and catch my breath.

I pull off my silk dress. Mostly naked, I lean back on my hands in the dirt and think about Sam. About that girl. "Kelly." Of course her name is Kelly. Kelly is always the cheerleader. The sorority girl. The blond lifeguard. Kelly.

Them talking in the bar. Him chasing after me like the arrogant prick he is, suddenly giving a shit if I'm all right.

I get my knife. I hold it for a while in the moonlight. I light my candles. The light flickers on the knife. So does the moon. I press my thumb into the tip.

I think about Sam in bed with that girl. I think about her saying his name.

My rage is greater than my hunger. Suddenly, I start stabbing the poor drunk. I stab him and stab him until I am covered in blood. Blood is everywhere.

I lick it off my fingers and feel spent and good. I feel like the monster I have become.

12

A love I'd kept
Died yesterday
As silently as sleep.

A painless euthanasia
There was no need to weep.

No one came in mourning
As I held it
Still and cold.

So all alone
I buried it.
In my churchyard, vast and old.

13

I welcome work this morning at the library.

Tucked in its dark corners, I read and stack and sort.

I hide. I eat lunch at my desk. I do not talk to anyone. I give Portia one-word answers until the end of the day. My eyes must look dead enough to scare her away.

At five p.m. I leave. I'm exhausted and just want to sleep.

When I get home, Sam is sitting on the hood of his car outside my house. He gazes down at the graveled road. "We need to talk."

"I don't want to talk to you."

"Too bad."

His hair catches the sunlight. I shield my eyes from it. It hurts.

"What the fuck, A.J.? What was that shit last night?"

"Please, just leave me alone." I sit on the steps.

I can't look at him.

He follows me to the stairs.

"How's your girlfriend?" My voice is quiet. I won't look at him.

"First, she's not my girlfriend. Second, she was really charmed by your act last night. Thanks for making such a good impression after all I've told her about you. And vice versa."

I look up finally. He takes a step back, looking into my eyes. He sees the deadness there.

"Do you think her opinion registers, even remotely, on the list of things I care about?" My voice sounds as dead as my eyes must look.

"Why are you doing this?" Sam says.

I cover my face with my hands.

"Talk to me. A.J. It's me. It's just me. Sam." He is pleading.

He kneels in front of me and pulls my hands from eyes.

"What's going on? Please tell me."

"I can't."

"You can. There's nothing you can say to me that would change how I feel about you. Don't you know that by now?" I'm so exhausted. So tired.

He lifts me into his lap and hugs me to him.

I wrap my arms around his neck in relief. I feel the sun coming from him in rays. He is warm.

I'm so cold.

"Sam." My head is on his shoulder.

"Yes?"

"How do you feel about me?"

My Blacksmith warned me not to ask. But I do anyway.

He pulls my head from his shoulder.

"Ainsley, don't you know by now?" He looks into my eyes. He pulls my glasses off. His hand strokes my cheek.

Then Sam is kissing me. It's a mistake. I can hear whispers coming from my graveyard.

Mistake. Mistake. Mistake.

The more open I am, the more horror he'll see. Turn back, I tell myself. But I don't. I am opening, slowly. I can feel my Blacksmith's anger. Jealousy. Disappointment. Mistake.

But I still kiss him. His tongue meets mine, and it's warm. I swallow his warmth. He makes me warm inside. Sam is the sun.

"Let's go inside." He opens the back door and leads me, still tired, almost stoned with exhaustion, confusion, and something else. The hunger lurches inside me.

Sam pulls me onto the couch and kisses me again. He is so gentle. I forgot what real kissing was like. He kisses me and rubs my back. I feel safe.

"Sam."

"Shhhh." He pushes me back onto the couch and pulls my sweater over my head. I open his shirt, still kissing him. We wrap around each other. I can see my yard from the window. I close my eyes. I ignore the whispers.

Sam holds me and warms me and I lose myself in it. I'm not a monster. I'm Ainsley. I am A.J. I am loved by Sam.

He fills me with his warm heart. I'm not so cold now. My mouth is buried in Sam's neck.

It's a mistake. But he holds me until I sleep.

When I wake, I'm cold again. I hold Sam to me, but I can't get warm. It's the middle of the night.

I know what I have to do. I've gone over it with my Blacksmith so many times.

"Sam...Sam, wake up."

He stirs next to me. He is so beautiful. Perfect.

He wakes up. He kisses me softly.

"Sam, I want to show you my garden."

"Now? It's the middle of the night."

"That's the best time. Come on."

I take his hand after he gets dressed, and we go up to the garden. "Jeez, it's dark back here."

"Don't worry, there's some light ahead."

We get to the graveyard. I find my matches and light the candles.

"Cool graveyard. But where is your garden?"

"This is my garden, Sam. I grow things here. I plant things here. I talk to the dead here."

He stares at me.

"I don't grow tomatoes, Sam. I'm not who you think I am."

"Ainsley, I think you're troubled. I don't know exactly what is going on. But it's nothing we can't fix together." He pauses. "Take my hand."

"I can't, Sam. It's too late for that. I'm a monster. Do you want to know who A.J. really is? Look back there. Behind the graves. Do you see those piles of dirt?"

He looks.

"A.J., I don't want to hear any more."

He backs away from me.

"I don't want to hear it. I don't want to know. Jesus. God." He sits down on my Blacksmith's grave. He covers his eyes with his hands.

The Blacksmith is whispering to me. He is telling me that he was right all along. I will lose Sam now. Forever.

There is only one way I can keep him. I can keep him always.

His eyes are closed.

I kneel before him, quietly. I'm crying. My tears water the soil.

"Sam."

"Don't, A.J. Don't." His voice is pleading. I think he is crying, too.

"Sam, look at me. Kiss me once more."

"I can't. I just can't."

"Please, Sam. You said you'd do anything for me. All I had to do was ask. I'm asking you for this one thing."

He looks up me. His eyes fill with tears. I've broken his heart. He is a victim of my dead, lurching hunger. I kiss his lips gently. "I'm so sorry, Sam."

Within me, my Blacksmith rages. I can feel him. This would prove his ultimate power over me. That he has won. If he can get me to sacrifice Sam for him, my evolution into a monster will be complete.

I pull out the knife.

And slit my own throat.

I love you, Sam.

Epilogue

They bury me in my graveyard. Sam sees to that.

They dig up my backyard. Body parts from eleven different men are recovered.

Some parts are missing, of course.

Sam has me buried where he knows I want to be. I'm not far from my Blacksmith. My headstone is a simple wooden cross. Sam keeps my name off the cross because he fears it would be vandalized or desecrated.

Sam visits me often. He is the only one.

Sometimes he cries. Other times he is angry.

But now, like me, he talks to the dead.

He sits on the bench for hours sometimes. Trying to understand.

I sit next to him, but he can't see me. I hold him when he cries and I comfort him. I touch his hair, in the sun.

f you pass by a graveyard, stop and walk among the dead. Don't be afraid.

Talk to them. They are lonely.

Even better, stop and see me. My grave is marked by a simple wooden cross. I am right near the Blacksmith. He keeps me company at night. We talk. I sit with the young Mrs. Brown, too. We talk about healing. About forgiveness. About motherhood.

I visit with the baby bird. My grandmother. The other A. All my friends, my lost ones, are here.

So stop and see me. I'd love to talk to you, too. I will hold your hand. I'm all right, now. I'm not alone anymore. The Blacksmith accepts me.

He has shown me how a dead heart can be made whole, when welded to another one just as lifeless.

My Blacksmith's fire burns within me—red and dead.

Come, sit by my Blacksmith and me. We will talk about love. But please, leave before dark.

And whatever you do, make sure you keep your voice down.

My babies are sleeping.